E $5.95
Hi   Hillert, Margaret
             I like things

I LIKE THINGS

A Follett JUST Beginning-To-Read Book

I LIKE THINGS

Margaret Hillert

Illustrated by Lois Axeman

FOLLETT PUBLISHING COMPANY
Chicago

Library of Congress Cataloging in Publication Data

Hillert, Margaret.
  I like things.

  (Follett just beginning-to-read books)
  SUMMARY: Easy-to-read text describes collections of familiar items which have been arranged by color, size, and shape.
  [1. Collectors and collecting—Fiction. 2. Color—Fiction. 3. Size and shape—Fiction] I. Axeman, Lois. II. Title.
PZ7.H558Iak [E] 80–21409
ISBN 0–695–41554–9 (lib. bdg.)
ISBN 0–695–31554–4 (pbk.)

Fourth Printing

I like things.
Big things.
Little things.
Red and yellow
and blue things.

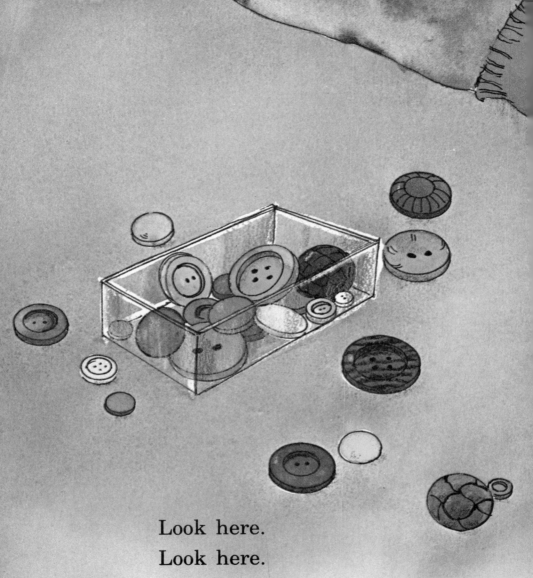

Look here.
Look here.
Here is something I like.
Something pretty.

Look what I can do.
Red, blue, yellow.
I can do it this way.
This is fun.

I can do it this way, too.
Big ones.
Little ones.

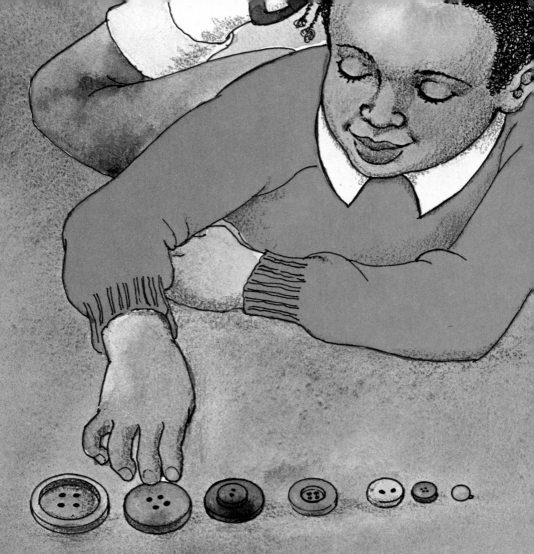

I can do it like this.
Oh, look at this.
This is a good way.

I can make something.
Something for Mother.
It is pretty.
Mother will like it.

Now here is something.
I like this, too.
Father helps me with this.

13

Oh, look.
Here are good ones.
Good ones for my book.

It is fun to do this,
but I have to work at it.
I find out things, too.
I like to do it.

Here is a good spot to
look for things.
I look and look.
What is here for me?
Guess, guess.

Now, look.
How pretty!
One can go here,
two here, and three here.

And I can do it
this way, too.
It is fun to play like this.

20

And here is something good.
I have things like this at
my house.

See this
 and this
  and this.

Look at the one in here.
See how this makes it look.
It looks big, and it looks
pretty.

My friend comes to my house
to see what I have.
This is fun.

He wants something that
I have.
And look at this.
I want this.

PEANUT BUTTER

GRAPE

STRAWBERRY JAM

Things are good to have.
But we want something to
eat, too.
Father will make something
for us.

We will go out to play now.
We will look for things.
We will find things.
What fun we will have!

I like things.
Big things.
Little things.

Red and yellow and
blue things.
What things do *you* like?

Margaret Hillert, author of many Follett JUST Beginning-To-Read Books, has been a first-grade teacher in Royal Oak, Michigan, since 1948.

I Like Things uses the 64 words listed below.

a	go	now	us
and	good		
are	guess	oh	want(s)
at		one(s)	way
	have	out	we
big	he		what
blue	helps	play	will
book	here	pretty	with
but	house		work
	how	red	
can			yellow
comes	I	see	
	in	something	
do	is	spot	
	it		
eat		that	
	like	the	
Father	little	things	
find	look(s)	this	
for		three	
friend	make(s)	to	
fun	me	too	
	Mother	two	
	my